How to Catch a Falling Star

Written by Heidi Howarth
Illustrated by Daniel Howarth

"What are you doing?" asked Hedgehog.

"Sitting and waiting for the star to fall," replied Bear grumpily. "The last star of the year."

"Oh. Can I wait, too?"

Bear said nothing. He just shuffled along to make a space.

And they sat and waited.

"What are you doing?" asked Mouse.

"Sitting and waiting for that star to fall," replied Hedgehog and Bear, pointing high up into the treetop.

"Oh. Can Rabbit and I wait, too?"

Bear and Hedgehog said nothing. They just shuffled along to make a space.

And they sat and waited.

Squirrel had been
watching from high in the
treetops. He had a wonderful idea.

"Don't worry, I can get it down for
you," he called. He reached out his paw...

"No!" cried Bear, Hedgehog, and Mouse.

Rabbit was too shy and said nothing.

"What magic?"

Squirrel stopped.

"Don't touch it!" said Bear. "If you touch it, the magic will be lost."

"Very strong magic, but not if you touch it!" shouted Bear.

Squirrel looked closely. The leaf looked the same as all the other leaves he had seen on the tree.

Squirrel scampered down the tree and rummaged through a pile of leaves.

"What is he doing?" asked Bear.

"I can't see," said Mouse. "I'm too small."

Bear smiled for the first time.
"Sit on my shoulder if you like."

Mouse was surprised.
"Thank you," he said.

No one noticed Squirrel
scampering back up the
tree. Now he sat there
with a leaf in his hand.

Silently,
he dropped it.

Bear gasped, Hedgehog shook,
Mouse squeaked, and they all
watched the leaf fall.

"We have to catch it,"
called Bear.

"We have to catch
the magic."

But where had it gone?

Still, no one had noticed Squirrel.
Suddenly his little tummy shook
as he let out a big chuckle.

They all looked up.

"It's right there," chuckled Squirrel.

"Behind you!"

Bear turned around,
but the leaf wasn't there.

Mouse and Rabbit turned around,

but the leaf wasn't there.

Hedgehog turned around,
but he couldn't see the leaf either.

Suddenly Bear, Rabbit, and Mouse started to laugh.

"The leaf's not behind you. It's on your behind!" they cried, pointing to the leaf on Hedgehog's prickles.

Bear looked sad.

"What's wrong?" asked Hedgehog.

"The magic is gone, and I needed it," cried Bear.

"But what for?" asked Mouse.

"To wish for someone to play with." Bear started to cry.

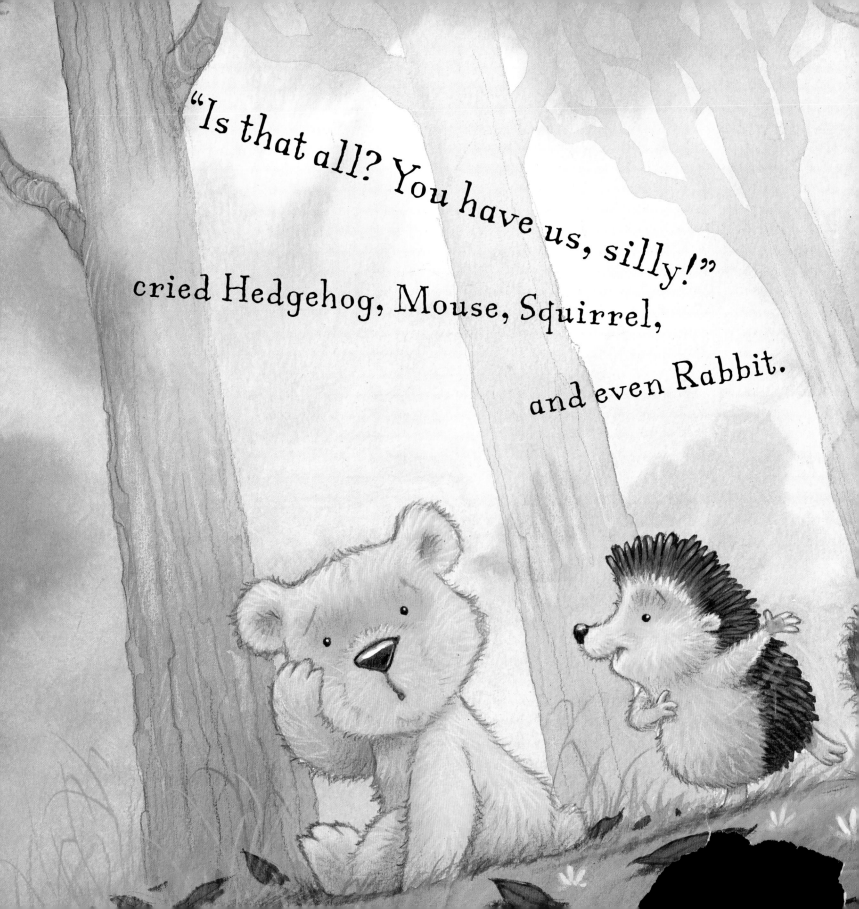

"Is that all? You have us, silly!" cried Hedgehog, Mouse, Squirrel, and even Rabbit.

And with that, the five friends
played together every day.

The magic of the leaf had worked.

Copyright © QEB Publishing, Inc. 2010

Published in the United States by
QEB Publishing, Inc.

This 2011 edition published by Sandy Creek by
arrangement with QEB Publishing, Inc.

ISBN 978-1-4351-3079-1

Printed in China
Manufactured December 2010

Editor: Amanda Askew
Designers: Vida and Luke Kelly

Sandy Creek
122 Fifth Avenue
New York, NY 10011

Lot 10 9 8 7 6 5 4 3 2 1

A CIP record for this book is available from the
Library of Congress.